Clementine
Friend of the Week

Clementine
Friend of the Week

SARA PENNYPACKER

PICTURES BY
Marla Frazee

𝒟ɪꜱɴᴇʏ • HYPERION
Los Angeles   New York

Text copyright © 2010 by Sara Pennypacker
Illustrations copyright © 2010 by Marla Frazee
The illustrations for this book were done with pen and ink on Strathmore paper.
Many thanks to Nadia Herman for her drawings on pages 64, 111, 155, and 156.

Printed in China
First hardcover edition, July 2010
First paperback edition, May 2011
10 9 8 7 6
Library of Congress Control Number for the hardcover edition: 2009004046
FAC-025393-16074
ISBN: 978-1-4847-8986-5
Visit www.DisneyBooks.com

This one is for The Great Cat Polka Dottie
 —S.P.

*To my cousin
Margaret, who
showed me Klickitat
Street*
 —M.F.

I couldn't wait for Margaret to get on the bus Monday afternoon. "It was the best day!" I told her. "I got picked for Friend of the Week! I get to tell my autobiography, be line leader, collect the milk money, feed the fish——"

"Oh yeah, Clementine," Margaret interrupted, flapping her hands at me. "We did that when I was in third grade."

Margaret is only one year older than I am. But whenever she says "When I was in third grade," she makes it sound like "Way back when I was a little kid, which I'm not anymore, so that makes me the boss of you." I want to learn how to do that trick in case anyone ever lets my little brother into third grade.

"Your class did Friend of the Week, too? I didn't know that," I said. "How come you never told me?"

Margaret crossed her ankles and looked down to see that her sock cuffs were matched up. When she looked back at me, her mouth was pinched like a raisin and she had turned a little pink. She shrugged. "I guess I forgot," she said. "I guess it was just too boring to remember."

"Friend of the Week isn't boring! Especially the booklet. Did you save your booklet? Can I see it?"

Margaret shrugged again. "My mother keeps it in the living

room. It's very important to her because it's all about my valuableness. I think she likes to have it around whenever Mitchell drives her crazy. I think she likes to read it and go, 'Whew! Thank goodness I have *one* good kid.' You probably shouldn't touch it."

"I won't hurt it," I said. "I'll be careful. Let's read it when we get home."

Margaret looked worried—like she was trying to think up something and couldn't—but then she shrugged a third time and said, "Sure, okay, sure, I suppose."

So when we got home, we rode the elevator down to my apartment to say, "Hi-Mom-bye-Mom-I'm-going-to-Margaret's-okay?-okay," to my mother. Then we rode the elevator up to the fifth floor, where Margaret's apartment is.

Margaret went straight over to the shelves next to the fireplace. She clasped her hands in

3

front of her, admiring the rows of trophies and awards she had won. Because we do this every time we're in her living room, I knew she wanted me to admire them, too. So I clasped my hands and we stood there having a moment of silence, staring at all the proof of how great Margaret was at everything.

There sure was a lot of it. Three whole shelves of "Best at This" and "Blue Ribbon for That" lined up all neat and tight like groceries in the supermarket.

I am really good at math and drawing. But nobody gives out trophies for those things, which is unfair. So all my parents have is a stack of math tests with stars on them, and some drawings taped up on the wall. They never put up a shelf in the living room for all my awards. Which is good, I guess, because it would be empty.

After I figured we were done with the admiring,

I went over to the shelves on the other side of the fireplace. There were lots of pictures of Margaret's older brother, Mitchell, there, playing baseball with his friends. And six identical baseball trophies. *M.V.P.* each one read, but with a different year. Nothing else.

"What does that stand for, *M.V.P.*?" I asked.

Margaret scratched her head like she was fake-remembering. "Oh, right! Moron-Villain-Pest," she said. "He wins it every year. No competition."

I knew Margaret was making that up because Mitchell isn't even one of those things. Which does N-O-T, *not*, mean he is my boyfriend.

I took a purple marker from my pocket and wrote *M.V.P.* on my arm with a lot of question marks after it so I would remember to find out what it meant. Margaret didn't notice because she had picked up a golden ballerina statue. "I

should have won silver and bronze statues for my other dances, too," she was saying. "But the judges didn't want the rest of the kids to feel too bad."

Now, Margaret can be kind of a braggy girl. But today she was being even braggier than normal. This could take a while. "How about the booklet?" I reminded her.

Margaret blew some invisible dust off the statue

and put it back carefully. She pushed aside a big spelling bee plaque on her bottom shelf and pulled out a blue booklet.

I reached for it, but she yanked it away. "Germs," she said, glaring at my hands. Then she sat on the couch and began to read.

"'It's good to have Margaret in our class because she is very organized.' 'I like having Margaret in class because she is neat.' 'Margaret is an extra-clean girl.'"

I sat down beside her and looked over, to see if she was fake-reading all those compliments. Nope, I saw with my own eyes—the page was full of stuff like that.

It's good to have Margaret in class because her hair is so shiny I can almost see myself in it! wrote Alexis. *I like sitting next to Margaret because she never lets her stuff spill onto my desk,* wrote Jamaal. And under that, Kyle had written,

Margaret is helpfull. Every day she tells me what I do wrong.

Margaret tapped the page. "I had to tell him he'd spelled 'helpful' wrong."

"Wow," I said. "That's a great booklet."

I started to get nervous. Even though I am

friends with everybody in my class, nobody was going to write anything like that about me, that was for sure. "What else did kids write?" I asked. "Anything about being a good draw-er, or good at math?"

"Just more nice compliments," Margaret said, jumping up suddenly. "Page after page. We should put it back now."

Margaret walked over to her shelves and closed the booklet. But instead of putting it back, she stared down at it and gasped. She turned red. If

her eyes weren't squidged down to slits, I bet I could have seen them boil. She looked like a cartoon person about to explode.

"That . . . that . . . that . . . that . . . OH!!!" she sputtered. Then she stomped out of the living room and down the hall and kicked open Mitchell's door. I followed her.

"Don't touch anything in here!" she warned me. "This place is crawling with germs!"

Mitchell was on his bed. He said hi to us from behind the sports section. Margaret went over to

him and stuck the booklet out, her whole body shaking.

Finally I saw what was making her so mad. On the cover of the booklet, someone had covered up the *r* in "Friend" with white tape.

MARGARET! the title read, above Margaret's smiling school picture. *FIEND OF THE WEEK!*

Mitchell made an innocent face and clapped his hands to his chest, like he was heart-crushed that she could accuse him of doing something like that. But I could see him telling his mouth not to laugh, and I could see his mouth fighting back.

"What makes you think it was me?" he asked, when he had won the fight with his mouth.

Margaret pointed to the baseball bat sticking out from under Mitchell's pillow. The handle was wrapped in tape that used to be white.

"Oh, yeah," he said. "I should have used Mom's nail polish or something."

Margaret stormed out of the room without saying a word and stomped back to her own bedroom. Her cat, Mascara, shot off the pillow and scrambled under the bed, because cats know when someone's mood is B-A-D, *bad*. Mascara and I waited while Margaret sat in the exact center of her rug and smoothed out all of the fringe, which is how she calms herself down.

"He is such a baby-head!" she hissed after a while.

"The cover's not important, Margaret," I tried. "Here, give it to me. I'll take the tape off."

Margaret clutched the booklet to her chest.

I almost pointed out that if Mitchell had touched it, it was crawling with germs now, but I didn't because I figured Margaret had been historical enough for one day. It didn't matter, though, because just then she figured it out for herself.

"Aaauuurrggghhh!" Margaret screamed. She dropped the booklet and ran into her bathroom,

waving her hands like they were on fire. I heard her turn the water on and start scrubbing.

Normally, Margaret and I never leave the other person alone in our rooms. This is because if Margaret is ever alone in my bedroom, her fingers get itchy to organize something. And if I'm ever alone in her room, my fingers get itchy to mess something up. As soon as Margaret went into her bathroom, I started looking around for what I could mess up. But this day, I saw something even better to do with my itchy fingers!

I reached under her desk, where her booklet had landed, and pulled it out. Very carefully—so carefully not one single speck of paper-skin came away!—I peeled off the tape.

Margaret came to the bathroom doorway then, patting the fingers of her left hand dry, one by one. "I have a good idea, Clementine," she was saying in a voice that sounded a lot calmer than the one she'd run into the bathroom with. "About how you can get a great booklet, like mine. Give everybody compliments all week. Then they'll give you some back in your booklet on Friday."

I held up her booklet, smiling. "Look, Margaret!"

"Or presents!" she said, as she started on her right hand. "Presents would be even better than compliments. And leave the price tag on, so everybody can see how good of a present it is and—"

"Margaret, look!" I interrupted her.

She looked up from her finger-patting. Her mouth fell open and she dropped the towel. She had that exploding-cartoon-person look again.

"Who said you could read that?!" she shrieked. Then she charged across the room and snatched the booklet from me, never mind the Mitchell-germs.

Mascara, who had stuck his nose out while Margaret was in her bathroom, skittered back under the bed. If I could have fit under there, I would have, too.

Instead, I was stuck trying to calm Margaret down. "I didn't read it! I was only . . . look! It's fine, the tape—"

"That was private! Anyone should know that! Anyone!" Margaret yelled.

"I only peeled the tape off, Margaret! I didn't hurt anything. Now, let's go back to the giving-presents idea, okay? You think people would write great stuff in my booklet if I give them presents?"

This is called Throwing Someone Off The Track. My parents say I am a genius at it, but it didn't work on Margaret.

"NOBODY'S GOING TO WRITE ANYTHING GREAT IN YOUR BOOKLET NO MATTER HOW MANY PRESENTS YOU GIVE THEM AND YOU'RE NOT EVEN MY FRIEND AND I ONLY PLAY WITH YOU BECAUSE YOU LIVE IN MY BUILDING AND NOW YOU HAVE TO GO HOME!" Margaret yelled at me.

"Well, well, well . . . OH, WHO CARES BECAUSE YOU'RE NOT EVEN MY FRIEND EITHER!" I yelled back. Then I ran out of Margaret's apartment and stabbed the elevator B-for-basement button so hard I probably broke it for life.

When I got to my apartment, my kitten was already waiting in the hall for me. That's how smart he is; he can tell it's me just from my footsteps.

I scooped him up and he gave me a kiss on my ear. "That's another way you're smart," I said. "You always know when I'm sad."

Then I draped him around my neck the way he likes, and carried him into my room, so I could tell him in private how mean Margaret had been to me. It took a long time, but finally I felt better. And as I sat there, patting his soft paws hanging over my shoulders, I realized something.

"Hey, Mom," I said, walking into the kitchen. "Look how long Moisturizer's legs are getting!"

My mom looked up from her carrot-peeling to see. "He's growing up," she agreed. "I've noticed that. He doesn't sleep as much these days—he's always exploring, getting into stuff. How was today?"

"Bad," I said, thinking about Margaret. I took a carrot and chomped it, hard. Then I remembered school. "And good, too."

"Which do you want to start with?"

"The good," I decided. "I got picked for Friend of the Week."

"Remind me what that is," Mom said.

But before I could, Turnip ran into the kitchen. He made a beeline for the pots-and-pans cupboard and dragged out the big spaghetti pot. He clapped it over his head and started whacking it with a wooden spoon, all the while laughing so

hard I could hear the drool bubbling up under his spaghetti-pot hat.

I patted Moisturizer to keep him calm during all the pot-whacking. And I tried to imagine what my brother's Friend of the Week booklet would say if he ever got to third grade.

"Mom," I asked, "do you ever wonder if Corn Kernel is normal?"

"First of all," my mother answered without stopping her peeling, "your brother's name isn't Corn Kernel. And second of all, of course not! What are you talking about?"

"Mom! Every day he takes off his shoes and then tries to put them on backward. Not just on the wrong feet, but backward."

My mom just shrugged.

"He thinks the washing machine is really a rocket ship."

Mom smiled.

"He *hammers rocks*. And even if he hits his head when he swings back, he keeps on doing it!"

My mom looked down at my brother as if she thought hammering rocks was the smartest, most adorable thing a person could do. "He does!" she agreed. "He'll do it for hours!"

Believe me, there were about a hundred more things I could have listed, but I stopped there because I didn't want to break my mother's heart about having such a disappointing second kid. I suddenly remembered what Margaret had said about how her mother likes to read her booklet whenever Mitchell drives her crazy. And that's when I knew. I was going to bring home a *wonderful* Friend of the Week booklet—so great it would make my parents' faces crack open with smiling pride. I was going to love showing them that booklet on Friday.

Okay, fine, I was going to love showing it to that braggy Margaret, too.

Just as I was enjoying thinking about Margaret reading all my great compliments, my dad came into the kitchen.

"Dad, I got picked for Friend of the Week—"

"Clementine, freeze!" he interrupted me. "Do not move one muscle."

"What is it—"

"Try not to panic," he went on, creeping up to me slowly. "I'll try to save you."

"Dad, *what?*"

"Don't look down now," he whispered. "But I think . . . I think your scarf . . . is *alive!*" Then he laughed and ruffled Moisturizer's fur and kissed my forehead.

"Now," he said, after he'd given my brother a kiss through his spaghetti pot, too, "what's this Friend of the Weak thing?" He flexed his arms. "Aren't you a Friend of the Strong, too?"

I laughed. "Friend of the *Week*. The seven-days kind of week. It's—"

My mother interrupted us by giving me a head of lettuce and the salad spinner and handing my father the spoon to stir the chili. This is because she is a really big fan of the Little Red Hen story. Anyone who expects to eat something in our house should expect to help make it. I always make a face about doing dinner chores, but the truth is I *like* being in the steaming, clattery jumble of dinner-making with everybody else.

So while my mother mixed the corn bread and my dad put his secret ingredients into the chili and my brother whacked more pots, I made a salad and finally told my parents about Friend of the Week.

"Every Monday, our teacher pulls a name out of a Kleenex box. That person, who is me this week, gets to be the leader of everything and tell about themselves. And everybody else has to say why it's so great to have that person around. The best part is that on Friday, they write it all down in a booklet for me to bring home."

"Excellent," my dad said. "I already know exactly what I'm going to write."

"Dad! Parents don't get to write anything. Only the kids." Then I started to wonder.

"Well, what would you write, though? I mean, if you could?"

"I'd write, 'I think it's wonderful to have Clementine in school because otherwise her mother and I would have no idea where the heck she was. If she weren't in school, that nutball kid would probably have her own television show, or she'd be running a tattoo parlor or dealing blackjack in a casino somewhere by now.'"

I have lived with my father for my entire life, which is almost three thousand days long now, and I *still* forget that he thinks he is a comedian. "Dad, that's not funny," I told him. "I wouldn't do any of those things until I'm big. Except . . . wait. What's a casino? What's blackjack? Would I like it?"

"Never mind," said my mom. "Clearly that's a very wise rule Mr. D'Matz has about only letting kids write in those booklets. And I can't wait to read yours on Friday. I'm sure we'll enjoy it."

"Enjoy it? You're going to love it!" I promised her. "In fact, you're probably going to want to build a whole shelf, right next to the fireplace, to keep it on!"

When my mom came in to say good night, she remembered there was a bad part to my day. "Want to tell me about that now?"

I shrugged and petted Moisturizer under the covers. "Margaret's mad at me. Really mad. And I don't know why."

"No idea?"

"Nope. She just went crazy. First at Mitchell, then at me."

"Well, maybe she's just having a bad day. But I'm sure you'll figure it out. You always do."

"You think so?"

"Sure. You two have been friends since the day Margaret moved in here."

"I thought we hated each other in the beginning. Remember? You told me Margaret was always trying to dress me up in her costumes and I hated that."

Mom nodded. "You'd run screaming when you saw her. You were about three. Then finally you'd let her stick a tutu on you, or a princess cloak, and then you'd go find a mud puddle to sit in." Mom laughed. "Yep, you were friends right from the beginning. So you'll work it out. That's what friends do."

Then she said good night and turned out the light.

In the darkness I held Moisturizer tight and thought about the bad news about that: Margaret and I *weren't* friends anymore.

3

Giving people compliments turned out to be a lot harder than Margaret had made it sound.

It started off okay on the bus ride Tuesday morning.

"That's a huge bruise on your arm! Great colors!" I said to Willy. This compliment made his twin sister Lilly smile too, because she had given him the bruise.

Then I moved over to where Joe was sitting. "You look a little taller today," I told him. "Maybe it's starting."

Joe is the shortest kid in our class. He's always

on the lookout for his big growth spurt, so this compliment should have made him happy. Instead, he looked puzzled for a minute and then hitched himself up and pulled out a lunch bag. Squashed. "Oh, rats," he said. "I hope it's not tuna."

And then, because nobody else from my class rides my bus, for the whole rest of the way I had nothing to do except ignore how Margaret was ignoring me ignoring her.

Things got harder in school. First my teacher said, "Clementine, as Friend of the Week, would you please lead us in the Pledge?" All I could think to do, standing under the flag, was give people the thumbs-up sign when they got the hard words, like "indivisible," right.

Next thing, it was my job to collect the lunch money and bring it down to the cafeteria. Let me tell you it is not so easy to compliment people about handing you money.

I told Waylon his quarters looked
especially shiny, and that he must keep
his pockets really clean. He liked that.
Next I told Maria that she counted her
change out really fast, but she said no,
it was just because I took so long
talking about Waylon's pockets.
Then I admired the way
Rasheed's nickels and
dimes were all stacked
up in one tall pile. He
said, "Thanks, it took a
lot of spit to get them to
stick together." Finally
I told Joe he had great
aim—like a much taller
person!—when he
tossed his money into
the envelope.

But that was it! The only other compliment I came up with was to the lunchroom lady who took the money. I told her that her hairnet made her head look like a hornet's nest from the back. She laughed and said, "Why thank you, girlie, now doesn't that just make my day!"

Which was nice, but it didn't really help because the lunchroom lady does not get a page in my booklet.

Back in the classroom, we did Circle Sharing Time and Morning Announcements, as usual. I spent the time trying to think of nice things to say to the kids. But then my teacher threw me off track.

"And finally, don't forget the bike rally Saturday to raise money for our third- and fourth-grade spring trip," he said. "I hope you're all decorating your bikes! See you at ten o'clock in Boston Common."

I could feel my inside face melting into a big secret smile, and I forgot all about the compliment-thinking-up.

My bike was going to look awesome on Saturday! In fact, I was going to have the best-decorated bike in the entire history of life. This is because the world's best decorations store is right in the basement of my building.

Well, not exactly. But my dad is the manager of our apartment building, and it's his job to decorate the lobby for holidays. He does the normal ones, of course, like Halloween and Thanksgiving and Valentine's Day. Boring, boring, boring. But my dad does his research and he says *every* day is some kind of holiday. Take January. Everybody knows about New Year's Day and Martin Luther King's birthday. But my dad also decorates for

Fruitcake-Toss Day, Punch-the-Clock Day, and Measure-Your-Feet Day.

Every week he posts what special days are coming up on the lobby bulletin board, along with suggestions for how to celebrate. For instance, April 30 is Hairstyle Appreciation Day, so in the elevator you might hear, "Mrs. Jacobi, what a lovely bun you're wearing!" Or Margaret's mother might compliment my mother on her tricky braid—but only if those things are true, since April 30 is also National Honesty Day.

"If I were in charge of the lobby at the UN, there would never be another war," my dad says. I think he's right—his holiday decorations make everybody happy.

Especially me. Because all these decorations live in our basement when it's not their turn. And when I asked my dad if I could borrow some for the rally Saturday, he said, "Sure, Sport, take them all if you want."

I still wasn't sure how I was going to decorate my bike, but that was only because I had too many great ideas. I felt my secret smile get even bigger. It's a good thing I know how to keep it from showing on the outside.

"Wow, Clementine," my teacher's voice interrupted. "You certainly seem excited to tell us your life story."

"Excuse me?" I asked. "What?"

"It's time to give us your presentation. That's quite a smile. I'm glad to see you're so happy about it. Come on up."

I looked through my backpack in case I had forgotten that I remembered to make some notes last night, but nope.

"That's all right," my teacher said. "Just come up and tell us about your life."

So I went up to the front of the class. "I was born," I began. And then nothing else came out, because it is very hard to think when you are standing at the front of a class with all those eyes on you.

"You were born," Mr. D'Matz repeated. "Where?"

"Here," I answered. Then all the kids started to laugh—but since it was a nice laugh, not a mean laugh, I laughed too. "No, I was not born in room 3B," I said. "I was born in Boston."

"And then?"

"And then I lived here, too. In Boston, not in room 3B. The end. Well, not *the end*, not yet. But that's all." I bowed and then started to head back to my seat.

The kids applauded, but my teacher stopped me. "Oh, I don't think that's all," he said. "I'm sure you've done lots of interesting things since you've been born. What do you think a biographer would say in a book about you?"

I shook my head. "Not much. I read two biographies this year. Did you know Harry Houdini was already a famous trapeze acrobat by the time he was my age? And Mozart had been composing music since he was five. Nobody could say anything like that about me."

And suddenly I had a great idea about why. "Those people back in ye olden times probably didn't have to go to school! Just last night, my dad said if I weren't in school I'd be doing lots of interesting things!"

"Well, you might indeed," my teacher agreed. "But for this presentation, let's just stick to what is. Now, wasn't there an addition to your family some time ago? Why don't you tell us about him?"

"You're right!" I cried. "I can't believe I forgot! Okay—I got a kitten at the beginning of the year, and his name is Moisturizer, and he's really smart and—"

"Well, actually, I was thinking about someone else," my teacher said. "Don't you have a younger brother?"

"Oh," I said. "Yes. I do. Broccoli. Now, one special thing about my kitten is that he's really—"

"Your brother's name is Broccoli? Seriously?"

"Well, no. But I got stuck with a name that's a

fruit, and it's not fair that he didn't, so I just call him vegetable names. Sometimes it's Corn, or Brussels Sprout, or Onion. It depends. Anyway, we've had him for three years now and he's kind of a disappointment, so I don't think I should talk about him."

My teacher laughed as if I'd made a joke. "Well, I think one thing we've learned is that Clementine has a good sense of humor," he said. "That's all the time we have right now. But for the rest of the day, let's all be reporters. Everyone find out one interesting fact about Clementine to share."

So, during recess the kids asked me questions.

QUESTION: If you were an animal, what would you be?

ANSWER: Gorilla.

QUESTION: What is your favorite color?

ANSWER: All of them.

QUESTION: Does your little brother do
any cute things?

ANSWER: No.

I was glad nobody asked me who my best friend was. Because I didn't have an answer for that.

4

After school on Tuesday I went straight to the basement.

The basement isn't really a basement—it's just the other half of the floor we live on, which is the bottom floor of our building. It is halfway below the sidewalk level and halfway above, so if you look out our windows, you see people's feet. My parents say living at this level keeps us grounded, and they laugh at that. I have noticed that grown-ups laugh at a lot of things that aren't funny.

Anyway, our apartment takes up half of the floor. The rest is what we call the basement—a huge space with the furnace and boiler in it, a workshop area, the building's laundry, and storage units.

My dad says being a building manager is like being the president, and that I'm like his vice president. Because I have to be ready to step in at any time, I know the basement almost as well as he does. So I knew right where the decorations were.

As I was pulling down the first box, labeled HALLOWEEN, I heard a little meow. "Hey, what are you doing out here? Want to help me decide about my bike?"

Moisturizer said yes in kitten language, so I dumped out the box in front of him—a bag of cobwebs and a bunch of big scary bats with black flappy wings.

Moisturizer corner-eyed the bats. He flattened himself and inched toward them, his nose trying to

48

twitch out
whether they
were real or not.
I slipped my hand into
the pile and flipped a switch on
one of the bats, so its red eyes flashed on and off.

Moisturizer shot sideways up into the air. His ears, his legs, and all the hairs on his tail spiked out as if every part of him was scared stiff. I knew he wasn't really afraid, though. He was just playing Captain Wonder-Paws—first he pretended to be the weak little kitten, then at any minute he'd change into the super cat.

Sure enough, he swaggered over to the bat and swatted it, and then turned away to flick his super tail, just to show it who was boss.

"Oh, Captain Wonder-Paws,"
I swooned, the way
he likes me to.

"You've saved us again! Also, you've helped me decide. I know just how I'm going to decorate my bike now!"

Moisturizer pretended to be too busy licking his shoulder to notice what a hero he was, and that was the end of his show. He curled up on the bag of cobwebs, and I left to get the umbrella I'd seen in the trash.

The umbrella was just the way I'd hoped—the tent was torn, but the skeleton was still fine. I ripped off the rest of the cloth, then went and got six bats. Luckily, the bats were already strung with clear lines, so all I had to do was tie them to the tips of the umbrella's skeleton arms. When they were all hanging, my dad passed by.

I held the swarm of bats over me, and he got the idea right away. "For the rally? You're going to attach it to your bike? Great idea. I'd use duct tape if I were you," he said. Then he untied the bat that

was in front of my face. "You have to be able to see, Sport, okay?"

And just then I had an even more spectacularful idea for that bat!

"Dad! On Saturday, could you pin this one across my shoulders, so it looks like it's biting my neck, sucking out all my blood?"

He grinned. "That would look pretty good," he agreed. "But you've got to promise to ride with both hands, that's the deal. Got it?"

I promised, and then I walked over to where my bike was stored.

Margaret's and Mitchell's bikes were in the rack, too. Mitchell's was covered with baseball-team stickers and looked like it had been through a bicycle war. Margaret's bike was purple and shiny all over—even the wheels. It looked beautiful, but it looked . . . plain. And then suddenly I had a wonderful idea!

I scooted Moisturizer back into the apartment,

and then I raced up to the fifth floor, smiling all the way—Margaret and I were going to be friends again!

Mitchell answered the door. He was holding a bowl of cereal and grinning. "Hi, Rugrat," he said.

Mitchell calls me names because he's trying to be my boyfriend. I don't tell him that I think, No, thanks! about having a boyfriend. I don't

want him to be too sad to play baseball.

"Margaret's in her room," he said. "Want to see something first?"

I said yes because suddenly I wasn't so sure I was ready to see Margaret's mad-at-me face. Also because if Margaret says, "Want to see something?" it's usually something boring, like a skirt she's picked all the lint from, or a new way she's lined up her barrettes. But if Mitchell says, "Want to see something?" you can bet it will be something good.

Except this time it wasn't! I followed him into the living room and he pointed his spoon to the bottom shelf. He started to crack up, but I didn't see what was so funny. Each one of his M.V.P. trophies wore a little triangle of paper towel with tiny pink safety pins at the tips.

"Margaret did that? Diapered all your trophies?"

Mitchell nodded, laughing. He wiped his eyes

with his T-shirt and took another grinning bite of cereal.

"Why aren't you mad, Mitchell? You love baseball. You're obsessed with baseball."

Mitchell put his spoon down. "Well, yeah.

Dude! I love playing baseball. But I don't care about the trophies."

When Mitchell said, "I love playing baseball," my heart gave a little jump, as if it were tired of sitting around in my chest and wanted to *go* somewhere. This is because Mitchell says the word *baseball* better than anyone in the world.

Then I asked him what I *really* wanted to know.

"Margaret has three hundred awards. Don't you mind that she's so good at everything? Doesn't it make you feel kind of . . ." I stopped and thought about how all those trophies made *me* feel. "Kind of . . . sorry for yourself?"

Mitchell looked at me the way I look at Spinach when he bangs his head inside the spaghetti pot. "I feel sorry for *her*." He waved his hand at Margaret's rows of awards. "I love playing baseball. Margaret just loves winning awards."

Mitchell picked up his glove and ball. "Gotta

go, Rugrat," he said. "Practice. Best part of the day."

I found Margaret in her room. She was swooshing around in a grass skirt with some plinky music on. Her arms looked like snakes, except not scary.

I said hi, and she said hi back, but that was it—no stopping the swooshing, no turning the plinky music off.

"I have a good idea, Margaret," I told her. "It's about the bike rally. You know how my dad keeps all those decorations in the basement? He says I can use them to decorate my bike. And you could, too! We could be a team—you could have bats swarming around you, like me—"

Margaret shot me a look that said, *Bats? Are you out of your mind?*

"Or whatever you want. Anything! I'm *sharing*! Want to come down and look?"

Margaret shook her head and kept on with her swooshing around. "Can't go to the rally," she said. "Competition Saturday morning. Have to practice my hula routine."

I reached over and turned off her music. "What do you mean you aren't going? You've been looking forward to it for weeks!"

Margaret stood there catching her breath for a minute. Then she said, "I can't go, Clementine. I have to go to the competition, or else someone else will win that trophy!" She snapped the music back on and started her routine over again, frowning this time.

My parents are always going on about the Golden Rule. "That 'Do' in 'Do unto others' can cover a lot of territory," they're always saying. My dad says it could mean, "Be quiet in the movies, as you would have others be quiet in the movies unto you." My mom says it could mean, "Don't interrupt people when they're drawing unless it's an emergency with blood, as you would have them not interrupt unto you when you're drawing unless it's an emergency with blood."

They use that Golden Rule on me a lot. But Wednesday, I got to use it on myself!

Here is how Wednesday went: After the Pledge and Circle Sharing Time and Morning Announcements, my teacher called for our attention. "Friend of the Week is a wonderful opportunity," he said as if he'd just thought of it, even though he says the exact same thing every week. "We're going to brainstorm a little bit now. Let's think about what makes Clementine a unique and valuable member of our class, so that on Friday we'll be ready to make her booklet."

He went to the chalkboard and wrote my name under the Friend of the Week sign. "Who'd like to get us started?"

I knew that all the kids were looking at me, so I tried to shine with valuableness. Since okay, fine, I didn't exactly know how someone would look when they were shining with valuableness, I did holiness instead.

Here is how you look holy: First—everyone

knows this part—fold your hands
like a steeple. Then roll your eyes
up as far as they will go, cross
them slightly, and let your
lids flutter a little bit. Finally,
imagine yourself doing something extra kind, like giving

away your ice-cream cone to a really skinny dog
even though nobody is watching.

The kids brainstormed about my good qualities,
and my teacher wrote their ideas on the board. I
listened—it was the regular stuff, about what a good
artist I am and how I notice interesting things—but
I didn't watch. Instead, I just sat there, steepling my
hands, crossing my rolled-up eyes, fluttering my
lids, and giving my ice cream to skinny dogs.

"Clementine, are you all right?"

I'd been concentrating so hard I hadn't noticed
my teacher sneaking up on me.

"For a minute you looked like you were going to faint," he said. "Would you like to visit the nurse?"

"No, I'm fine," I said. And I wasn't even embarrassed, because while I was doing all the looking holy, I had decided to give up on giving compliments and try giving presents. And the Golden Rule good idea had come to me: *Give tattoos unto others as you would have others give tattoos unto you!*

During geography, I made my sign: TATTOOS, FREE TODAY—USUALLY $40!! Then I added another

zero so everyone would know this was a really great present.

At recess, I tucked my markers into my pocket and went out with my sign. I stuck it into the fence far away from where the teachers patrolled to make sure the sixth graders didn't murder each other in dodgeball, and waited.

The first person to come over was Charlie. "Free tattoos," I told him. "I usually charge four hundred dollars."

"My uncle has a naked lady on his arm," Charlie said. "She's sitting on an anchor."

"I don't think I can draw a naked lady," I told him. "I never did that before."

"That's okay," Charlie said. "I don't want one. I just wanted to tell you that." I thanked him and then drew an anchor on his arm. I added a fish sitting on the anchor.

"It's naked," I told him.

The next person to come over was Rasheed. He said he never thought about what he would like for a tattoo . . . did I have any suggestions?

"Well," I said, "I like to draw reminders to myself on my arm." I showed him the one I'd added Monday.

"'M.V.P.', Most Valuable Player," Rasheed read.

That Margaret.

"That's a good one, I'll take it." He rolled up his sleeve. "Never mind the question marks, though."

Lilly wanted her usual picture—a rainbow with three tulips under it. I sit next to Lilly in class, and I'm getting pretty tired of that rainbow and those tulips. I tried to talk her into something more interesting. "How about a plate of spaghetti and meatballs under that rainbow?" I suggested. "How about a zebra eating those tulips?"

But Lilly doesn't have much of an imagination.

She shook her head. "I'll stick with the rainbow. But I guess you could make it four tulips if you want to."

Lilly's twin brother Willy wanted his usual, too. I didn't argue with him, because I like drawing zombie sharks, even though he insists on lots of pointy teeth and I am not so fond of pointy things. I figured they were on his arm and not mine. I drew extra gently over his new bruise so the shark was all green and purple and black, and he loved it.

Things kept going pretty well until Maria came up. "I want a baby goat," she said. "We went to a petting zoo last summer and I saw one there."

Even though I am a really good artist, I was stumped. A baby goat was probably the one thing in the world I had never drawn—besides a naked lady—and here she was asking for it. Finally I had a solution.

"What's that?" Maria asked when I was finished. "What's all that scribbling? What are all those dots?"

"That's a bush," I explained. "The baby goat's inside, eating berries."

"Wow," Maria said. "You're an even better artist than I thought!"

Norris-Boris-Morris-Horace-Brontosaurus was next. His real name is Norris, but in the beginning of the year I couldn't remember that, so I gave him all the "orris" names I could think of. He loved

that. For a minute I was afraid he wanted me to tattoo them all on his arm, but nope.

He rolled up his jeans. "Make my legs trees," he said. "With bark and leaves and stuff. And put some acorns in, too. So when my grandmother makes me go to the park and sit with her while she knits, squirrels might run up my legs."

I thought that was a good idea. But now there were a lot of kids lined up behind him. "Sorry, Norris-Boris," I said. "Tree legs would take too long."

He sighed and rolled up his sleeve. "I don't care, then," he said. "Draw whatever you want."

I drew some peanuts on his arm. "When you're at the park, lie down on the sidewalk," I explained. "Pigeons will land on your arm and peck."

Norris-Boris-Morris-Horace-Brontosaurus went away smiling, and I started smiling, too. That was going to look pretty good in my

booklet: *Clementine is a good friend because she helped me get pigeons to land on my arm.*

Margaret didn't have anything like that in her booklet, that was for sure.

CHAPTER
6

As soon as recess was over, my teacher sent me down to the principal's office with a note.

Mrs. Rice read the note and shook her head. "Didn't we just go through this, Clementine?"

"No. The thing with Margaret's head was a long time ago—at the beginning of the year. Besides, this is different. For one thing, the kids *wanted* me to draw on them. For another thing, none of them has Margaret's mother for a mother. So it's going to be fine."

Mrs. Rice sighed. "How about this. How about, the next time you decide to share your artistic talents with your friends, you do it on paper?"

I didn't want to embarrass Mrs. Rice by pointing out that tattoos don't work very well on paper, so I just said, "Sure, next time I will. Thanks for the great idea." Then I told her the great idea *I'd* had.

"You think students should have professional-development days, the way the teachers do?" she asked, even though I had just said exactly that.

"Right. Some extra days off to get better at stuff. So if anybody wants to do a biography about us, they'll have something to write about."

"And you would come to school to do it, the way the teachers do?"

"Well," I said—slowly, because I had forgotten to think about this part. "Maybe not. Maybe we'd go to Jack's Joke Shop. Or a casino. Someplace where we could learn some interesting things."

"Well, Clementine," said Mrs. Rice, "I could run that by the school board. But I think I already know what they'd say."

"What?"

"I think they'd say you students already have professional development days. Two of them a week. They're called Saturday and Sunday."

Then Mrs. Rice swiveled her chair away from me and clutched the top of her head, with her shoulders shaking. I knew she was secretly laughing, so I said I was all done visiting her, and I left.

One thing they do not teach in principal school: what is funny and what is not.

After school on Wednesday, my mom walked me over to Maria's apartment to play, because she was working on a big illustration job. Inside, she thanked Maria's mother for having me. "Next time, bring Maria over to our place," she said.

Maria's mother said, "That would be lovely; next time for sure, the girls can play at your place."

Maria and I made faces at each other under our mothers' arms, because both of us knew that was never going to happen in a million years. This is because Maria's mother doesn't allow Maria any place where there's a television set she might get a glimpse of.

"For Pete's sake," I once heard my mother complain to my father. "What does she think we're watching over here, *Forbidden Secrets of Juvenile Delinquents?*"

"That's ridiculous, we would never watch that," my dad said. "Because *Trashy Tales of Hollywood Hoodlums* is on at the same time."

My mother laughed and tossed her paint rag at him, but then she said, "Really, though. What's the problem?"

I knew what the problem was. Maria's mother

thinks watching any television at all, even PBS, rots your brain for life, so it's no TV for Maria.

The good news, though, is that they let her do lots of other things instead. As long as it isn't watching television, they are yes-saying parents.

Maria took me into her room and pointed to an aquarium. "Look! There's my new lizard! My parents let me have him because nobody mentioned the head lice time in my Friend of the Week booklet last week. Isn't he great?"

He was great all right! He was climbing the glass wall so you could see all the little suction cups on the bottom of his feet. His tongue was darting in and out, tasting the glass, about a hundred times a second.

"Wow! That's a wonderful pet!" I said, and I wasn't even trying to compliment her. "What's his name?"

Maria bent down and pressed her face against

the glass where her lizard was sticking. She stuck her tongue in and out really fast, too. "He likes that," she told me. "We're talking. I don't know what his name is . . . I haven't figured it out yet." Maria began blinking her eyes fast, and her lizard did the same. He was a really good pet, all right.

"Oh, I can help you with that!" I cried. "I'm an expert at picking pet names."

And it wasn't just bragging either. Because I have discovered something—the best names in the world are on labels in bathrooms. I took the most beautiful word ever invented for my own kitten's name, but there are plenty of good ones left.

So I said, "Show me to the bathroom, Maria." And I guess it was a lucky day for all three of us— me, Maria, and her lizard—because right away my eyeballs snapped over to the perfect word as if they were suddenly made of steel and the jar on the top shelf was a magnet.

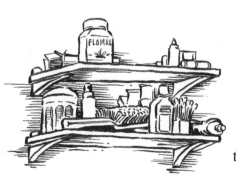

"Maria," I said, "your lizard's name is Flomax."

Was she ever happy! She could hardly stop thanking me!

"No problem," I said. And then I added, "It was just one of the unique and valuable contributions I like to make!"

I was in for at least one good page in my Friend of the Week booklet.

Which wasn't the reason I helped her.

Okay, fine, it wasn't the *only* reason I helped her.

Next, Maria took me out to see her bike.

"How are you going to decorate it for the rally?" I asked.

Maria laughed. "You're funny, Clementine! It *is* decorated!" She made *Tada!*-arms over her bike, and I looked closer. There were a few playing cards stuck in the wheel spokes and some crepe-paper streamers hung from the handlebars. That was all.

Maria got on and rode around me a couple of times. "How'd it look?" she asked when she got off. "Great, huh?"

Maria feels bad enough being the only kid in our class who can't watch television, so I didn't tell her that the only thing that looked great to me was the baby goat eating berries in a bush on her arm as she whizzed by.

This made me feel really happy about how

wonderful my bike was going to look at the rally. But it also made me feel a little bit sad about that, too.

And that's when it hit me—an idea for an even better present than tattoos to give everybody!

It was a good thing I'd had my spectacularful idea, because Thursday morning nobody even mentioned my tattoo presents.

"I forgot about it," Lilly said at recess. "I guess it washed off."

"Mine too," Willy agreed. "You should have used permanent markers."

And that is how unfair the world is. When I colored on some hair for Margaret and me, I was in trouble because I used permanent markers. Now here I was in trouble because I *didn't* use them. Although . . .

"Um . . . Nobody is mad at me, right?" I asked.

"My uncle might be," Charlie said after a minute. "I showed my mom how my tattoo was like his, and she called him up in Ohio and hollered at him so loud she didn't even need the phone. He can never come for a visit again unless he wears long sleeves, taped down at the cuffs."

I figured Charlie's uncle didn't count, since he wasn't going to write in my booklet. The important thing was that none of my classmates was mad at me. Norris-Boris was a little disappointed because his tattoo hadn't worked, but that was all.

"Two hours and fifteen minutes lying on the sidewalk in the park yesterday afternoon," he sighed.

"And no pigeons?"

He shook his head. "Not even one. Three ants, though—big ones. So it wasn't a total waste."

After that, nobody even talked about my tattoos

because they were too busy talking about their bike decorations for Saturday, which were all as boring as Maria's—playing cards, streamers, and a couple of balloons.

So it was the perfect time to tell them all about my new present idea!

"Come to the rally early," I said. "Don't bother decorating your bikes at home." And then I explained about my dad's stuff and how I would bring it all to the Common.

That got their attention, all right. They glued all thirty-six of their eyes on me like they were seals at the aquarium, just waiting to see where the trainer was going to toss that fish.

"So I can have anything I want on my bike?" asked Joe. "What does he have?"

"Anything. Whatever you can think of, he's got it."

"How about tulips and a rainbow?" Lilly asked.

"Spring decorations," I answered. "No problem, Lilly."

"How about a zombie shark?" Willy asked.

"That's harder," I admitted. "There is no National Zombie Shark Day. But for National Fishing Week, my dad hangs big rubber trout from the ceiling. We can tape some sharp teeth to one of them."

That made Willy really happy. As we lined up, I told the kids about more of the great stuff my dad had, they told me what they wanted, and by the time we got back into the classroom, *everybody* was happy.

Especially me.

As soon as I got home, I found my dad in the basement. "Did you really mean it, I could use *all* your decorations for the rally?"

He nodded. "Sure. But it will be a little

hard to fit them all on one bicycle, Sport."

"How about *nineteen* bicycles?" And then I told my dad the plan.

Which he loved. He got as excited as I did, pulling out all the things we could use.

When I told my dad about Norris-Boris's wanting to be a tree, he said, "Piece of cake. Squirrel Appreciation Day," and he pulled out some oak branches and a stuffed squirrel.

And that was just the beginning—we went right down the list like that, taking care of everyone in my class.

Pretty soon, Mom came in with Yam and a load of laundry.

"Free . . . two . . . *ONE!!!*" my brother shrieked when he caught sight of the washing machine. He climbed up onto the dryer and

pulled down the rocket-fuel detergent.

My mom put the clothes in the washing machine and then looked over at all the boxes. "What's up?"

So I explained the plan to her, too.

"Free . . . two . . . *ONE!!!*" Chili Pepper hollered as he leaned over and cranked the dial.

"That's so nice of you, Clementine!" Mom said. "To share your artistic talents with your classmates like that."

"And to share all these valuable resources, too," my dad said. "Let's not forget them! And, you"—he turned to point at me—"don't you forget to get all this stuff back."

"Now, Bill," my mom said. "What would be the harm if a few things got lost?"

My mom is the only person in our building who does not enjoy my dad's decorations. This is because they are plastic—because of fire codes—

and plastic is like kryptonite to all-natural people like my mother. She practically has a heart attack if she just hears the word "artificial." She swept her hand over the tulips we'd pulled out for Lilly, then squeezed her eyes shut as if it hurt to look at them.

My dad threw his hands out over the tulips as if he were showcasing the top prize on a game show. "Are you kidding?" he asked. "Just look at these colors!"

"Exactly," my mom said. "Look at them! These colors do not exist in nature. How about, if just for once, we had real flowers in the lobby?"

"Fire codes," my dad said with a pretend-sorry

face. "What can we do?"

"Oh, for heaven's sakes," my mom said. "Give me one example of a pot of daisies bursting into flame and burning down a building!"

My dad spread his arms out to show how helpless he was, and my mom rolled her eyes. And then they both started laughing, which made me start to laugh, and then Turnip joined in from the top of the washing machine. Suddenly Moisturizer appeared, and I think he was laughing, too.

I scooped him up. "Hey, you're back out here? Didn't want to miss any fun?" I asked him. "Well, you can help me decorate my bike, I guess."

Mom and Mung Bean left, and I was just about to ask my dad about blood for my neck, when Roberta the delivery woman stuck her head in. "Hey, hi, Pony Express!" she said to me. Then she nodded to my dad. "Four packages, supposed to be on the loading dock. You know anything about that?"

My dad left to help her look for the packages, and I finished draping my bike with cobwebs. My dad came back in, but before I could show him, Franklin the electrician showed up. "Hi, Sparky," he said. "I need your dad. Got a call about a short circuit up on the sixth floor." And then my dad was gone with him.

Next to come in was George the plumber. "Hey, Squirt," he said. He put down his tool bag and told me plumbing stories until my dad came back to take him up to the fourth floor for a leaking dishwasher.

A little later, just as my mom and Radish came in, Dad came back. "Welcome to Grand Central Station," he said. "You guys have tickets?"

"Better than that," my mom said as she pulled the clothes from the washing machine and stuffed them into the dryer. "We're here to tell you the dining car will be serving in ten minutes. How about you start packing up so you can come in for dinner, all right?"

So I stuffed everything into garbage bags and tied them up, ready to go Saturday morning. "Here, Moisturizer," I called. "Want to eat?"

He didn't come, so I went and looked everywhere I remembered seeing him.

No kitten.

"Hey, Squash," I said, "Have you seen Moisturizer?"

"No kitty," my brother said. "Blast off?"

"He's probably inside the apartment," my mom said. "We're having macaroni and cheese. He's probably sitting by the stove, drooling." She picked up Potato and headed into the apartment. I followed her and called for Moisturizer again.

He didn't come. I grabbed the box of kitty treats and went around the whole apartment shaking it and calling his name. "He always comes for treats, so he's got to still be out in the basement," I told my mom in a voice that was a little

shaky. "I'm going to go get him."

Back in the basement, I called and I shook the box, and I called and I shook the box. I walked around, opening doors and cupboards and boxes, and the bags of decorations. I looked in all the washers and dryers, in the storage room, in both elevators, in the trash barrels and recycling bins.

"Here, kitty! Moisturizer, here!" I called, faster and faster. I could feel my heart start to beat faster, too. "Where *are* you?"

My dad came out. "No sign of him?"

Suddenly my throat squeezed down. I pressed my lips together and shook my head.

"Okay," he said. "Let's be calm. Let's think like a kitten here." And then he began searching in all the building-manager places he could think of— the garbage chute, the old closed-up coal bin, the air shaft, the air-conditioning unit. He shined a flashlight into the heating ducts and behind the hot-water tank and under the furnace. He even opened his toolbox.

I followed him, calling Moisturizer's name and shaking his treats.

No kitten. *No kitten!*

My heart started to pound so hard I was afraid I might not hear him if he meowed for me. "Dad," I cried finally, "what if he got . . ." I took a deep breath but I still couldn't make my mouth say the next word.

Dad squatted down in front of me and put his

hands on my shoulders. "I don't think he did that, Clementine," he said. "I think he's just on a little adventure. The basement is a pretty exciting place if you're a kitten. He's just found something more interesting than his dinner right now. So let's go eat ours, and I bet when we're done, he'll show up."

I said okay, but when I got to the table, it was N-O-T, *not*. Not even one macaroni would go down—my throat closed just thinking about how much I wished Moisturizer was under the table right now.

"Can I take my plate to the basement?" I asked my parents. "So he'll smell it and come home?"

They said okay, so I did. One by one, I laid the

cheesy macaroni elbows on the basement floor, making a trail through all the places we'd been, ending up at our door. Then I went calling through the basement again, begging Moisturizer to come out, and keeping one eye on the trail.

But Moisturizer didn't come. And then I knew.

"Mom, Dad!" I cried as I ran back inside. "He got *out!*"

CHAPTER
8

We split up. My mom and I went north, and my dad, wheeling Cabbage in the stroller, went south. Then we went east and they went west. No kitten. Block after block after block. Just too many cars and trucks and taxis and buses—all of them big and fast and none of them watching out for a lost kitten. I stopped everyone we passed and asked if they'd seen him: "Little and orange and fluffy and smart?"

"No, sorry," everybody said. "Sorry, no."

We searched until the moon was high in the sky and Boston was falling asleep. Finally, my parents said, "Your brother's been conked out for hours and it's getting cold and it's time you got to bed, too, Clementine. Moisturizer is probably asleep now anyway, so we might as well go home."

At the lobby door, I called for him one more time while my dad carried my brother inside. My mom stood beside me. "It's a really big night out there, Mom," I told her. "And he's a really little cat."

"I know, honey," she said. "I know."

Inside, I dragged my quilt and pillow out to the living room and spread them on the floor beside the door.

"Clementine, I don't think . . ." my mom started.

"If he's in the basement and he comes back, I need to hear him," I said. "Besides, I can't sleep in my bed if he's not there." I thought I would have to use my stingray eyes to convince her, since she's usually a bedtime-is-a-time-not-a-feeling-and-we-sleep-in-our-own-rooms kind of mother. But tonight she just hugged me and asked my dad to get the air mattress for me and sleep on the couch beside me.

My dad blew the mattress up. Then he went outside and scratched at the door, to make sure I could hear if Moisturizer came home. The sound made the tears I had been holding back all night burst out.

"Hey there," my dad said, closing the door and sitting beside me. "You can't give up hope. Moisturizer is counting on you. Wherever he is, he's not giving up hope."

I wiped my face. "Do you think he knows I'm coming to find him tomorrow?"

"Absolutely. From the moment I set eyes on that cat, I thought to myself, 'That cat is positive. That cat is not a quitter.'"

"But now he's all alone in the world without me, Dad! It's dark and it's cold, and he thought I would take care of him and I didn't!"

"I think you do, Sport. Your mother and I noticed that. We never have to remind you to feed him—never, not even once. He didn't get out because you were careless. He got out because he was curious. Kittens are curious."

That reminded me about a certain terrible saying about curiosity and cats, which I am not going to repeat. I saw my dad see me remembering it. He wrapped his arms around me just as I burst into tears again.

"'But satisfaction brought him back.' That's the end of that saying, remember," he said.

"I hope so, Dad," I said into his shoulder. "Because I really want him back."

CHAPTER

9

I don't want to talk about Friday because there was so much crying. I did not know one person could hold that much water. That's all I'm going to say about that.

Okay, fine, I'll tell about *some* of Friday. The parts that weren't as bad.

I must have missed Moisturizer while I slept, because I woke up crying. My parents took one look at me and called the school to say I wasn't coming in, which was good because I had decided that already.

I wiped my face. "Okay, let's get going," I said.

"Let's start searching for him again."

"Hold on," said my dad. "I think we can be a little smarter than that. Let's get some more people looking."

"You're right!" I cried. "Let's call the police, and the FBI and the CIA and—"

My dad didn't call the FBI or the CIA because he didn't think a crime had been committed. But he did call the police and the Animal Rescue League and the vets in the area. Then he told me the best part of his plan—posters! Which sounded like a great idea, until I thought of something terrible. "Oh, no! We never took any pictures! I forgot to take pictures of him!"

More crying. My dad put his arm around my shoulder. "That's a challenge, all right. But you know what I think? I think Moisturizer is one lucky kitten right now. Because he belongs to a remarkable artist."

"You think I could draw him?" I asked. "You think I could do a good enough job?"

"I do, Sport. I think it will be the drawing of your life."

"Me too," said my mom. "But first, let's get you some tissues. You can't splash tears on a drawing this important."

So I dried my tears and then my mom let me sit up at her drawing table to make the poster. She handed me her good markers and a stack of her good paper. "Use as much as you need, honey," she said. "Get it right."

Let me tell you, it was very, very hard. Not the drawing part. The not-crying-on-the-paper part.

When I tried to draw his ears, I remembered how they twitched whenever someone opened a can, and my eyes filled up. When I drew his fluffy fur, I remembered how soft it was to pet, and the tears ran down my face. And when I sketched in his whiskers, I thought about how sometimes he walked around with little dust bunnies on them, and I almost fell off the chair from crying so hard.

Okay, that's enough about the crying!

Finally, what I did was repeat over and over while I drew, "This cute kitten is coming home soon! So I am very happy!" I held a tissue up to my eyes with my left hand while I drew with my right, just in case.

I had a little problem deciding what expression to put on Moisturizer's face. I love it when he's curious, but also when he's laughing, and also when he's yawning. In the end, I decided to make him look a little afraid, because that's how he'd probably look when a stranger found him.

Finally, the drawing was done. And look how good it was!

I added our phone number to the bottom, and then my dad and I walked to the copy shop on the corner.

"How many would you like?" the clerk asked.

"How many can I get for this much?" I asked back. And I put all the money I owned on the counter.

My dad scooped it up and gave it back to me. "This one's on me," he said. "Now how many posters do you think we need? Fifteen, twenty . . . ?"

"A hundred," I said.

"Oh, I don't think a—" Dad started.

"You're right," I interrupted. "Two hundred. No—three hundred. At least."

My dad looked at me hard for a minute. Then he turned to the clerk. "Three hundred copies, please. This is a very special cat."

* * *

Let me tell you, it is a lot of work to put up posters, especially when you have a three-year-old brother trying to help. Luckily, Parsnip decided around lunchtime that it was more fun to stick tape on himself than on the telephone poles, so we got a lot more done in the afternoon.

"How many do you think we put up?" I asked my mom as the afternoon faded.

She eyed the stack. "Maybe fifty?"

"Well, only two hundred fifty left," I said. "Let's get going."

Mom shook her head. "Your dad is working. He can't answer the phone in the apartment. We should go home in case someone calls."

So we went back, and my brother peeled tape off himself, and my mom made dinner while I sat by the phone and waited for someone to call.

Nobody did. Well, except for a stranger who wondered if I had enough mortgage protection. I told him about Moisturizer being gone and he said, "Oh dear, that's a shame, I hope you find him real soon."

After that, the phone didn't ring at all. And the whole apartment was quieter than it had ever been before—it was missing the sound of the phone *and* the sound of Moisturizer being there.

When it was time for bed, I dragged the air mattress over to the door again. My dad went to read my brother his bedtime story and my mom came out with a pillow and a blanket. She lay down on the couch. "I thought you could use some company," she said, and she shut off the light.

"Mom," I said into the darkness after a while. "You know how Pea Pod says, 'You broke my feelings,' when he means they're hurt? Well, that's how I feel—like all the feelings inside me are broken."

"I know just what you mean," my mom said. "I think that just about sums it up. But they'll be fixed again, I promise."

"How do you know?"

"You're a human being, right? Human beings have feelings. Everybody feels that sad sometimes. People write stories about it, and poetry; they paint pictures and compose music about it. To share how it feels."

I didn't answer. Nobody in the world could ever have felt the way I did right then.

"For instance," she went on, "do you remember last year when we read *Ginger Pye* out loud? Remember how those kids felt when their dog was missing?"

I nodded into the dark.

"And do you remember how long it took to find him? And how they never stopped looking, and how finally, finally, they got him back?"

"Mom," I said. "That was a book. This is real life."

CHAPTER

10

Early Saturday morning I heard knocking. I sat up and my ears got excited—maybe someone had found Moisturizer! I jumped up and opened the door.

It was just Margaret.

"Is your dad home?" she asked. "It's my big recital today. I need the storage keys so I can get— Hey! Did you go blind? Is that why you weren't in school yesterday?"

"What are you talking about?"

"Your eyes! They're red and all swollen. They look like tomatoes."

"Never mind," I said. My dad was in the kitchen making breakfast with my mom. I told him Margaret needed him, and then I ran into my room and flopped onto my bed.

After a few minutes my dad came in and sat beside me. "Did you tell Margaret about Moisturizer?"

I kept my head buried in the pillow as I shook it.

"She'll be back in a few minutes with the keys. It might help. To talk to a friend . . ."

"Margaret isn't my friend. She's mad at me and I don't even know why, and she said my eyes look like tomatoes."

My dad rolled me over to look. Then he made a pretend horrified face.

I laughed a little, even though I didn't want to. "Anyway, she's on her way to her big hula-dancing recital—she won't want to talk to me.

Besides, if she did, she'd just tell me it's my fault. She never loses anything. She'd tell me I shouldn't have lost Moisturizer."

"She might surprise you. Maybe you should give her a chance."

I sighed and went to the front door. Margaret came back in a few minutes, dragging a giant blow-up palm tree under her arm. She handed me my dad's keys and started to leave. Then she turned around. "I saw your bike," she said. "It looks good."

"The rally! I forgot!" I wailed. I felt my chest hitching up for another day of crying, so I wrapped my arms around myself to keep it all in.

"So what?" Margaret said. "You have time. Go get ready. And wear sunglasses."

"I can't. *I can't!*" And then, when I was trying not to say why I couldn't, the words all came out.

"Moisturizer's gone?" Margaret gasped. *"He's gone??"* Then her face got all scowled up again, like it did when she was so angry at Mitchell and me the other day. Even her palm tree looked furious.

I ran back into my room and threw myself onto my bed again. After a minute, my dad came in. "Well," he asked, "did Margaret surprise you? Did it help to talk?"

"Yes, she surprised me," I said, after I thought about the way she had acted. "But no, it didn't help. Dad, I let everyone down, everyone."

He sat down on my bed. "What are you talking about?"

"I let Moisturizer down by losing him. And you and Mom—I let you down because you gave him to me. Right now, I'm letting everyone down about the rally. And Margaret—you should have seen her face."

"You've never let us down once, Sport. That's
not how your mother and I see all this." He nodded toward the kitchen. "We've got a pancake

factory out there. Come on out and eat some. Maybe you'll feel better."

I shook my head.

"You've got a big morning ahead. A lot of posters to put up. I think you should eat something."

So I got up and ate some pancakes, even though they all reminded me so much of Moisturizer I might as well have been eating cat food. One looked like his head and another like his tail, and the rest looked like his paws. Probably everything from now on was going to remind me of him.

After breakfast, my mother and I put on our jackets. "Oh dear," Mom said, frowning down at the table beside the door. "Margaret asked me for some posters as she was leaving, so I took a few out and left them here for her. But she must have taken the whole envelope by mistake." My mom saw my face and quickly made a smile. "She'll bring them back. Let's take these few for now and get started."

Five posters. We put one up in the lobby and then there were only four. We walked around all morning, calling down alleys, looking under cars and behind trash cans and up trees. We put up the four posters, which didn't take long. I was so sad about that, I didn't pay attention to which way we were going home.

And then suddenly we turned a corner and I saw them right across the street—a huge group of kids clustered together with their bikes on Boston Common.

"Mom, run!" I said, grabbing her hand and pulling her away. "I can't let them see me! They're going to be so disappointed with me!"

"Wait," she said. "Let's go talk to them. Let's explain what's going on. . . ."

But I couldn't. I couldn't bear to see their undecorated bikes and their Clementine-let-us-down faces. I ran all the way home.

When I got there, I decided I couldn't bear to

see the trail of crusty lumps of macaroni and cheese anymore, either. I got a spatula and a plastic bag and started scraping them off the floor. It took a long time because they had hardened like cement. As I was finishing up at my doorway, Margaret got out of the elevator. Holding a big manila envelope!

"Oh, thank you!" I cried.

She came over to give it to me, but she stopped when she saw what I was doing and arrow-eyed my hands. She opened our apartment door and put the envelope on the table instead. One nice thing I have to admit about Margaret—she takes good care of everything, not just her own things. So I knew the posters were going to be just fine.

"Did Moisturizer come home?" she asked.

I shook my head. "Did you win the competition?"

Margaret shook her head.

"But you win everything, Margaret!" I said.

"I know." Margaret shrugged. "I didn't enter."

I was so surprised I just stared at her. "But . . ."

"I had something else to do. And besides, a hula

skirt is made of grass, Clementine," Margaret said, as if this explained it. *"Grass!"*

"What's wrong with grass?"

"Hel-*lo*?" Margaret said. *"Grass-germs??"* She rolled her eyes and shuddered. Then she turned and pressed the elevator button. "I have to go now. I hope you find your cat."

I went inside and washed the macaroni cement off my hands. Then I found my mom. "Margaret brought the posters back. We can put them up now."

My mom said just a minute while she finished her work, but it was really about two hundred minutes. Finally she came out and picked up our jackets. I opened the envelope.

There were no posters inside. Just a thick blue booklet.

CLEMENTINE: FRIEND OF THE WEEK! the cover read above my school picture.

I dropped the booklet. My mom picked it up. "How nice," she said. "Let's read it."

"Mom!" I wailed. "The kids wrote about me on Friday! Back when they thought I was a good friend because I was going to help them decorate their bikes. But I didn't show up at the rally, so now they think I'm their Enemy of the Year, not their Friend of the Week!"

I took the booklet and ran into my room and

threw it under my bed. My dad calls that space The Black Hole, and for once, I wished he was right— I wished things disappeared under there forever.

Then I ran up to Margaret's.

Mitchell answered the door. "I saw your sign in the lobby. Moisturizer's gone? Dude, that's just *wrong*. I'm going to a friend's, but if you haven't found him by the time I get back, I'll help you look."

I thanked him and asked for Margaret.

"She just left with our dad," he told me. "She'll be back tomorrow night."

"Well, I don't really need her," I told him. "Just my posters—she took all my Missing Kitten posters by mistake. Do you know where they are?"

"I saw Margaret when she got home—no posters, Rugrat. Just that giant palm tree."

"She didn't bring them back? Are you sure? I need them!" I felt my tomato eyes start to fill up again, and I scrubbed at them so Mitchell wouldn't think I was a baby.

"She took your posters? Dude. I'm her brother. It's her job to be mean to *me*. But she likes you, Clementine. What did you do to make her so mad at *you*?"

"Nothing! I touched her booklet—that's all! I peeled off the tape you put on it, and when I tried to show her, she thought I was reading it and she went nuts."

"Oh, her booklet," said Mitchell, as though that explained everything.

"But I didn't read it, Mitchell! And anyway, it's not a diary—it's not private. I didn't do anything wrong! And she's so mad she got rid of my posters? So mad she doesn't want me to find my kitten?"

Mitchell was quiet for a minute, and I could see he was trying to decide about something. "Okay.

Don't tell her I told you this, Rugrat, but . . . her booklet is practically empty. She's embarrassed about that—there are only a couple of pages of stuff in it. That's all the kids could come up with—a couple of pages."

"Oh. Oh." And I couldn't think of anything else to say as Mitchell waved good-bye and told me he hoped I found my cat.

CHAPTER

I I

That night, my whole family slept in the living room with me. But on Sunday morning, my mom rolled out her yoga mat and my dad went out for bagels and the *Boston Globe*. After breakfast, he lay on the couch with the paper and my brother crawled up beside him, pretending to read the comics.

I couldn't believe it. My family was acting as if this were just a normal day in our normal lives.

"Excuse me," I said, really loud even though the rule is quiet for Sunday morning yoga and paper reading. "Excuse me, but someone is *missing* here."

"Not much we can do about that today, Sport," my father said. "The police and the Animal Rescue League have the info, and we put up posters. Now I think we just wait it out."

"*Wait it out?* You mean *stop caring?* What if it were me? Would you just *wait it out* if I were lost?"

"Of course not," my dad started.

"Well then, let's go. Let's get looking for him, let's make some more posters and put them up."

"Your dad's right, honey," said my mom. "It's pouring rain out, so even if we got more posters made, there's no point in putting them up. Besides, I bet Moisturizer's in someone's home right now. He's probably fine. We aren't going to find *him*—whoever has him has to find *us* now. So we just have to wait it out."

I didn't answer. I was never going to speak to anyone in my family for the rest of my life. Margaret either, of course. I brought a pad of paper and a pencil into my bedroom—the only thing I was going to do for the rest of my life was draw pictures of Moisturizer. I was going to be like that famous artist in New Orleans who only paints one thing—a bright blue dog. I always wondered why that artist only painted that one dog, but now I knew. He must have missed that dog a lot.

I got to work on my drawing: Moisturizer pouncing on a shadow. As I drew, I tried to picture what my mom had said—Moisturizer, fine, in someone else's house. At first that made me feel better. But then I started to wonder. What if there was another girl in that house? And what if Moisturizer started to love her? And what if he forgot all about me?

I suddenly thought of one day last week, when Moisturizer had wanted to sit on my lap and I hadn't let him. Mitchell and his friends were skateboarding in the alley, and I went out to watch them instead. What if Moisturizer remembered that and *wanted* to love a different girl? A girl who would let him sit on her lap forever?

That made me mess up the drawing, so I tore it up and started a new one—*my* kitten on *my* pillow, looking *happy*.

After a while the phone rang, and I ran to answer it. It was only Aunt Claire, wondering if it was currants or raisins in the coffee cake my mom brought over the other day. I told her Mom was doing yoga, and I thought chocolate chips would taste a lot better anyway. Then I told her about Moisturizer being gone. All she said was, "That's too bad, I hope you find him, and have your mother give me a call. I want to make that coffee cake for my book club Tuesday." So I was never going to speak to Aunt Claire again, either.

I went back into my room and started another drawing in my soon-to-be-famous "Orange Kitten" series: *Moisturizer Napping on the Windowsill.*

My dad knocked. I ignored him. He came in

and brought a section of the paper over to me. "Look at this."

I shook my head and kept on drawing.

"I really think you should look, Sport," he said.

I pressed my mouth into a ruler line because suddenly not talking to my father made me want to cry.

He put the paper down next to my drawing.

I corner-eyed it, just a peek. I looked again. And then I picked it up to study it, in case my eyes were playing tricks. There, right on the front page of the *Boston Globe* Living Section was my Missing Kitten poster. Underneath was a picture of my school's bike rally. All the bikes were covered with sheets of paper.

My dad held my hand while I read the headline: *STUDENTS USE BIKE RALLY TO HELP FIND MISSING PET!*

Just then my mom came in with Lima Bean.

"We wondered where everybody was. . . ." she began. Then she saw the paper, too.

My dad read the article out loud.

"'Missing Kitten posters covered nearly a hundred bicycles in a fund-raising rally on Boston Common, after a concerned student alerted her schoolmates to a friend's situation . . .'"

"A concerned student?" my mom asked. "Who?"

"I don't know. The only one who knew was . . . but she was . . . no . . ." I said, confused. "But she had the posters, and that explains how she got my booklet. Besides, look, here it says the concerned student organized the whole thing. *Organized!* It had to be Margaret!"

"Margaret," we all repeated. *"Margaret!"*

"This is wonderful!" my mom said. "Hundreds of people—maybe a thousand or more—saw those flyers!"

I was so happy. I couldn't get over what Margaret had done. Just when I thought she was being the meanest to me, she was being the nicest.

But then I realized something. "That was yesterday. A thousand people found out about Moisturizer yesterday. But nobody called."

"But thousands more will find out about him today, from the paper, Sport," my dad said. "I think it's just a matter of time now."

The day took three hundred hours. I checked the newspaper to make sure the right phone number was in the story, and I checked the phone every few minutes to make sure it was working. I stood by the window watching for little kitten paws to walk by in the rain, until my legs ached. And I did a lot of drawings of Moisturizer: stretched out in the sun, swatting a fly, tangled up in ribbons, falling into the garbage can. Each one

made me miss him more.

My family went on acting like it was a normal Sunday, I went on watching out the window and drawing my kitten, and the phone went on not ringing.

Until late in the afternoon, finally, finally it did.

My mom picked it up. She listened for a while, and a smile grew on her face. For just a minute I was mad at her; how could she smile on a day like this? Then I heard her say, "I think the person you want to talk to is my daughter."

I grabbed the phone.

"I have a kitten here," said a man's voice on

the other end. "A very curious kitten. I saw the article in the paper and wondered if he's the one you're looking for?"

"Is he . . . ?" And then my throat squeezed shut from how much I wanted it to be Moisturizer.

My mom saw that I couldn't talk. She took the phone again. She hoisted me up onto her hip like I was three years old, and I didn't even care about that; I just listened while she talked.

"Is he orange and fluffy, about four or five months old?" she asked the man. "Does he look really well taken care of?"

I buried my head in my mom's neck, and I was shaking too hard to hear the man's answer.

"That sounds like him," my mom said. "Where do you live?"

My mom listened and then her whole body slumped. "Oh," she said. "Oh, that's too bad.

The kitten we're looking for was lost in Boston
Thursday night. I don't think he could have gotten that far. . . ."

My mom looked at me with an I'm-sorry
face. I looked back at her with an I-don't-

care-we-have-to-find-out-anyway face.

"It's probably not our kitten," my mom told the man on the phone. "But let me get your address—we'd like to take a look."

My dad drove me, and all the way there he kept warning me not to get my hopes up. "This kitten showed up on his doorstep Thursday night," he said. "In Quincy. That's almost fifteen miles from here. Even if Moisturizer could walk that far, he could never have gotten fifteen miles in just a couple of hours." I tried not to listen to him.

Finally we got to the address. We knocked on the door. A man answered. In his arms was a kitten.

"*George!*" my father cried to the man.

"*Squirt!*" George the plumber cried to me.

"*Moisturizer!*" I cried to my kitten.

Moisturizer jumped into my arms and then we all talked at once, figuring out what had happened.

"It never occurred to me!" George kept saying.

"I got home Thursday night, took out my key to unlock the door, looked down, and there was this kitten. I figured he was from around here. It never occurred to me he might have been in the van."

"He must have climbed into your tool bag," I said. "He loves exploring."

"He's been pretty curious here, too," George said. "Cute little guy. Peppy. I'm going to miss having him around. But I guess I can visit him sometimes, now can't I!"

We drove back home with Moisturizer draped around my neck. He purred into my ear until he fell asleep, which was probably because he was exhausted from pretending to be happy in someone else's house.

My dad glanced back at us in the rearview mirror and pretended he'd been blinded. "I wish I'd brought my sunglasses," he said. "They might as well shut the power down in Boston—you could light up the whole city tonight with your smile."

I laughed, but secretly I flashed my smile around the backseat, and he was right, it did light things up.

Mom had dinner waiting, and she pretended not to notice that I snuck Moisturizer little bites of meat loaf under the table. Afterward, my parents asked if they could read my Friend of the Week booklet. I said okay and crawled under my bed to get it. We all went into the living room.

The booklet was full of long paragraphs about stuff I hardly remembered doing.

Once, when I was in first grade, I lost my crayons, Joe had written. *Clementine broke every one of hers in half, so I could color.*

Waylon wrote, *I like having Clementine in class because she believed me when I told her about my superpowers. She is the only one I will teach how to become invisible—as soon as I learn how.*

It's good to have Clementine in class because you

always know we will be laughing, wrote Willy.

His twin sister Lilly wrote it was good I was there, *because otherwise my brother would be in trouble the most.*

And Maria's page said, *When my mom found out my lizard's name, she said, "That child has been watching television!" And my dad confessed that sometimes he let me watch golf when she was at bingo, and then she said, "Oh, fine, I give up, I guess she's old enough to rot her brain if she wants to." So, thanks to Clementine, I can watch TV now!* Which just goes to show you that you never know when you're doing a good deed.

None of the kids even mentioned my promise to decorate their bikes! But a lot of them did say they appreciated how I shared my artistic abilities. Which made me feel guilty for a minute about letting them down Saturday. But then it gave me an astoundishing idea.

"Pet portraits!" I told my mom and dad. "That's how I'll thank them for helping me find Moisturizer! One for every person in my class. I'll draw their pet, or, if they don't have one, I'll draw the pet they want to have someday."

I got started right away. First I did one for Margaret, because I wanted to thank her best of all. I drew Mascara curled up in the big straw hat I'd decorated for Margaret once, which is his favorite place to sleep.

Next I did a beautiful portrait of Flomax for Maria—up on the glass aquarium wall with his tiny foot suction cups showing, and dashes in the air around his tongue to show it

Flomax

darting in and out. Then, for the rest of the kids, I wrote out fancy "I.O.U. One Pet Portrait" certificates.

My parents came to take a look. "That's so nice of you, Clementine," my mom said. "Your classmates are lucky to have you for a friend."

My dad put my Friend of the Week booklet on the fireplace mantel, between my parents' wedding picture and the baby pictures of my brother and me. "We want it right up here," he said, "where

I.O.U.
One Pet Portrait

everyone can see it and know how proud we are of you."

And then suddenly I had another wonderful idea.

I ran to the phone and called up Mitchell. "Is Margaret home yet?"

"She just got back," he answered. "Batten the hatches, matey."

"Can you sneak her Friend of the Week booklet out for me?"

"Sure!" said Mitchell.

This is a great thing about Mitchell. Whenever you ask him to do something, he says "Sure!" even if it's something he could get in trouble for. If I ever want a boyfriend—which I will not—he will say "Sure!" to anything I suggest.

Mitchell was down in a few minutes. He grabbed Moisturizer from me and high-fived his paw. "Little dude! You're home!"

Then he followed me to the kitchen table and

watched as I flipped the booklet open and started to write: *Margaret is the best friend a person could ever have!* And then even though my hand was exhausted from drawing all those pictures of Moisturizer, two pet portraits, and seventeen I.O.U. certificates, I wrote and I wrote about what she did on Saturday. I filled up her booklet and I didn't even have to write extra big.

"Margaret did that?" Mitchell asked, reading over my shoulder.

"Yep," I said.

"The Margaret who's my *sister*?"

"That Margaret," I said. "Let's go put it back now. I'll do it so you don't get in trouble."

I hung Moisturizer around my neck, because I didn't feel ready to leave him for even a few minutes. Then we went up in the elevator, Mitchell muttering all the way, "My sister did that? *Margaret?*"

We hurried to the living room. Margaret wasn't in sight, so I pulled out the spelling bee plaque and was just about to tuck the booklet behind it, when I heard her voice.

"You got him back! You got him back!" She ran over and hugged Moisturizer while I stood frozen. Then she looked down.

She turned pale. She took the booklet from me, trembling.

"I did not read it," I said quickly. "N-O-T, *not*. I'm sorry I took it, but I only wanted to write something. I wanted to thank you . . ."

Margaret shushed me. She opened the booklet and began to read. She scowled and then she nodded and then she scowled again and she nodded again. Lots of times.

Finally she looked back at me. "Grateful just has one *l*, Clementine," she said. "And hero just has one *e*. And there were only 239 posters, not 250. And—"

I felt a little bit relieved. "Do you want me to take it out, Margaret? I could erase it all if you want. . . ."

Margaret tipped her head and narrowed her eyes, as if she were thinking about it. But her mouth kept twitching up, so I could tell she was just pretending. Finally she gave a big sigh. "Oh, I suppose, if it means that much to you, Clementine, we could leave it in. *Okay, fine.*"

And then she put the booklet away—but this time, not on the bottom shelf behind the spelling

bee plaque. This time, Margaret put her Friend of the Week booklet right up in the middle of the fireplace mantel.

And then she turned and smiled at me so brightly the whole city of Boston actually did light up. Okay, fine, maybe my smile helped too.

If you enjoyed this book, look for the next Clementine adventure!

CHAPTER

I

The very first thing Margaret said when she sat down next to me on the bus Monday morning was that I looked terrible. "You have droopy eye bags and a pasty complexion. Absolutely no glow. What's the matter?"

"I'm having a nervous breakdown," I told her. "Our *Family Meeting!* sign is up and I have to wait until tonight to find out if I'm in trouble."

"Of course you're in trouble," Margaret said. "Probably something really big. Bright pink blush and a sparkly eye shadow is what I recommend."

This winter vacation, Margaret had visited her father in Hollywood, California. When she got back, I had to listen for three hundred hours to how great his new girlfriend was. "She's the makeup artist for his commercials," Margaret said all melty-voiced, as if she was the one who was in love with this Heather person.

"Someone who puts makeup on people isn't an artist," I informed Margaret. "My mother is an artist. Not her."

"Heather is too an artist," Margaret snorted. "And she's been teaching me some of her professional techniques." Then Margaret had blabbered on and on about advanced lip gloss tips and the proper application of eyeliner until I thought I would die of bore-dumb.

"I don't need any blush!" I yelled at Margaret,

a little louder than I meant to. "I don't need any makeup at all! I just need to know what I'm in trouble about!"

Margaret rolled her eyes at me and then dug around in her pocketbook. She pulled out a pointy silver tube that looked dangerous, like a bullet.

"Margaret!" I gasped. "Are you putting on lipstick?"

Margaret smeared the lipstick on and pooched her lips out and smucked them at me. "Yep," she said. *Smuck-smuck-smuck.* "So what? I'll take it off before we get there."

"Mar! Ga! Ret!" I cried. *"You are ten! Years! Old!"*

Margaret had had her tenth birthday while she was on that vacation in Hollywood. Since then, she had been acting like she was twenty-five or something. Sometimes I didn't even recognize her. Plus I didn't get to go to a party for her.

Margaret smucked her shiny pink lips at me again. "Heather says I am very mature for my age." She waved the lipstick tube in front of my face. "You want some?"

I tapped my lips. "Mouth germs," I warned her. "I can feel them crawling around."

Margaret yanked the lipstick back in horror and then spent the rest of the bus ride wiping everything in her pocketbook with hand sanitizer. Being a germ-maniac was about the only thing I recognized about the new Margaret.

I opened my backpack and pulled out my *Important Papers* folder and found a good surprise: The science fair project report Waylon and I wrote was still in there! It doesn't always happen this way.

As I started reading over the paper, I calmed down. This is because lately I really like science class.

I didn't always. In the beginning, science class was a big disappointment, let me tell you.

On the first Monday of third grade, Mrs. Resnick had started talking about what a great year it was going to be.

I looked around the science room.

No monkeys with funnel-hats and electrodes. No alien pods leaking green slime. No human heads sitting on platters under glass jars talking to each other, like I'd seen in a movie once, and don't bother telling my parents about it because I was grounded for a week already and so was Uncle Frank who brought me to the movie.

No smoking test tubes, no sizzling magnetic rays, no rocket launch controls. Just some posters on the walls and a bunch of tall tables with sinks, as if all you would do in a room like this was wash your hands. Margaret had told me she liked science class, and now I knew why: Margaret says, "Let's go wash our hands," the way other people say, "Let's go to a party and open presents."

"Does anyone have any questions?" Mrs. Resnick had asked that first day.

I sure did—I wanted to ask, "You call this a science room?" But instead, I just said, "Excuse me, but I think there's been a mistake," in my most polite voice.

"A mistake?" Mrs. Resnick asked.

"Right," I said. "I'm in the wrong science room."

"The wrong science room?" she asked.

I nodded. "I want the one with the invisibility chamber and mind control buttons and mutant brains spattered on the ceiling. The one with the experiments."

"I want that one, too," Waylon said. I gave him a big smile.

"Oh, there are plenty of experiments going on

here," Mrs. Resnick said. "We're going to have quite a year."

Mrs. Resnick seemed nice, so I didn't tell her the other bad news: that she had the wrong hair. Scientists are supposed to have wild science-y hair, and hers was just kind of normal supermarket-y, television-mother-y kind of hair. Probably she was embarrassed about that.

Now, though, I like science class. I like the project we're doing for the science fair, and I like our rat, Eighteen. I like that I got Waylon for a partner. All the kids begged him to be their partner, because he's the scienciest kid in third grade. But he picked me, because I'm the only one who believes he's going to be a superhero when he grows up.

And today, I had an extra thing to like about science class: for forty whole minutes, I wouldn't have to think about our family meeting or Margaret's lipstick smucking.

IF YOU ENJOYED THE
CLEMENTINE BOOKS, LOOK FOR

Waylon!
One Awesome Thing

SARA PENNYPACKER

PICTURES BY
Marla Frazee